Holly Jolly Jimmy

Based on the TV show *The Adventures of Jimmy Neutron, Boy Genius®* as seen on Nickelodeon®

SIMON SPOTLIGHT
An imprint of Simon & Schuster Children's Publishing Division
1230 Avenue of the Americas, New York, New York 10020

Manufactured in the United States of America
First Edition 10 9 8 7 6 5 4 3 2 1
ISBN 0-689-85846-9

Holly Jolly Jimmy

adapted by Adam Beechen
based on the screenplay by Gene Grillo
illustrated by Natasha Sasic

Simon Spotlight/Nickelodeon
New York London Toronto Sydney Singapore

It was Christmas Eve in Retroville.

For show-and-tell at school, Carl brought half-eaten cheese nibs. "I put them out for Santa last year," he told the class proudly. "See? This one even has his teeth marks."

"I think your parents ate those," said Jimmy Neutron. "I don't believe there is a Santa. How could he fit down a chimney or live somewhere as cold as the North Pole?"

Later, in his lab, Jimmy used a monitor to show Carl and Sheen a bright star. "Two years ago I asked Santa for a piece of this dwarf star," he told them. "When I didn't get it for Christmas it was the saddest day of my life, and I started to wonder if Santa was real."

"Maybe you were naughty," suggested Sheen. "Wasn't that the year you almost blew up Earth?"

Jimmy showed them how it wasn't possible for a reindeer to fly and that presents for all the world's children couldn't fit into even the largest sack.

He pulled down a chart
covered with a long equation.
"I've run the numbers, guys.
THERE IS NO SANTA CLAUS!"

Moping, Carl sat on Jimmy's scanner. It suddenly came alive with a Christmas energy pattern!

"It must be the cheese nibs in your pocket," Sheen said excitedly. "I bet they set off the scanner because they're covered with Santa's DNA!"

"We'd have to see the same pattern at the North Pole for me to believe it's Santa," said Jimmy.

"Let's go!" Carl shouted.

They loaded Jimmy's rocket with supplies and took off for the North Pole. "Santa Claus, here we come!" Carl shouted joyously.

Soon the boys landed at the North Pole. It wasn't long before Sheen saw a sign for Santa's Workshop.

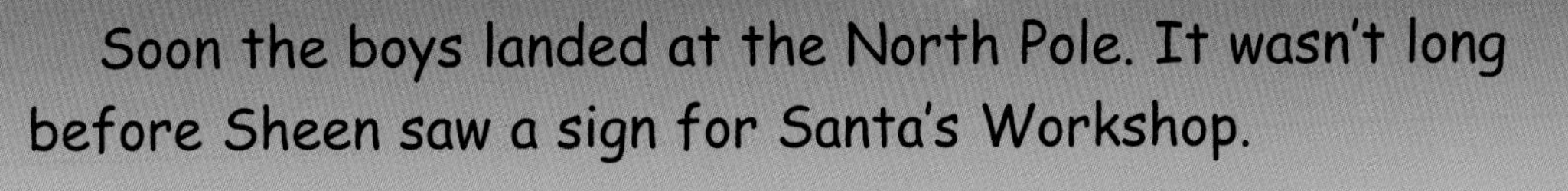

"My scanner is showing that Christmas pattern again," said Jimmy. "Come on!"

When Jimmy and his friends arrived at Santa's Workshop they found lots of elves—but no Santa!

"It's Christmas Eve," the head elf told them. "Santa's getting ready!"

But Jimmy didn't believe it.

"This whole thing is a sham, guys," he said to his friends. "This is just a fancy warehouse!"

"But what about the elves?" Sheen wanted to know.

"Short guys with ear conditions," explained Jimmy, shrugging.

"We prefer 'diminutive helpers,'" corrected the head elf.

"The only thing I can't figure out is this strange energy pattern," said Jimmy.
"Don't play with that scanner in here," the head elf warned.
"Relax," Jimmy told him. "What could go wrong?"

Just then a bolt of energy shot from the scanner, bounced around the room, and flew out the window into a nearby cottage, where it zapped the man who lived inside. "Ho, ho, ho—OUCH!" the man cried out.

A red phone rang in the workshop. The head elf answered it. "Oh, no," he said after listening for a moment. "That's terrible!"

He hung up the phone and turned to Jimmy. "Santa's atoms have been scrambled! We have to cancel Christmas . . . and it's all your fault!"

"I didn't hurt Santa, because he doesn't exist," Jimmy shot back. "I think you're just covering up because I figured out your scheme!"

"We'll still have Christmas," Jimmy told them all. "I'll deliver every last present."

"Who do you think you are?" the head elf wanted to know. "Santa?"

"No, just a normal kid," Jimmy replied. "And if a kid can deliver all the world's Christmas presents using science, you'll all be forced to admit that there is no Santa Claus!"

Sheen whispered to Carl, "The Easter Bunny is still real, right?"

Soon Jimmy had upgraded his rocket. He put jingle bells on the engines, attached a navigational beacon to Goddard's nose, and loaded the hypercube with presents.

"You'll never make it," the head elf said. "You've got to deliver presents to every kid on Earth, and you only have twelve hours to do it!"

"We'll make it," Jimmy assured him. "Jingle bells to speed!" The rocket roared off into the Christmas Eve night.

Jimmy flew his rocket all over the world.

Carl and Sheen took turns tossing presents down chimneys.

"We're almost done . . . and right on schedule," Jimmy said hours later.

"When you tell everyone we brought their presents, people will know there's no Santa Claus," Carl said sadly.

"Cheer up," Sheen told him. "We'll be heroes in Retroville!"

"Holy Heisenberg!" Jimmy exclaimed. "We still have to bring presents to Retroville!"

Jimmy quickly attached a Warp Module to his console.

The rocket ship reached light speed, but only for a moment.

"The strain is too much," Carl yelled. "The ship's coming apart!"

Jimmy, Carl, Sheen, and Goddard fell toward the Earth.

"This is quickly becoming a really lousy Christmas," Sheen pointed out.

Suddenly a deep voice called out, "Holly Jolly Tractor Beam . . . ACTIVATE!" An energy beam caught the boys and Goddard and stopped their fall!

Jimmy and his friends looked up to see that Santa and his sleigh had saved them!

“Santa, you *are* real,” Jimmy said, amazed. “I’m sorry I scrambled your atoms.”
“It took Mrs. Claus hours to restitch them together,” Santa told them.

"Can you still bring Christmas to Retroville, Santa?" Carl asked.

"I'm afraid that rescuing you used up all my reserve energy," said Santa.

"But you can do *any*thing!" Sheen pleaded.

Santa thought for a moment. "Brain Blast! I need a Warp Module!" cried Santa.

"Goddard has a spare," Jimmy said, taking the module from one of Goddard's compartments.

Santa attached the module to his sleigh, and they zoomed away!

Santa's sleigh raced over Retroville as the sun rose.

Santa steered while Jimmy and his friends tossed presents down chimneys. They finished with only moments to spare!

"Thanks, Santa," Jimmy said. They had already dropped off Carl and Sheen, and now it was Jimmy's turn.

"No problem, Jimmy," Santa answered. "Stay off the Naughty List!"

Santa's sleigh sped away.

"What a nice guy," Jimmy said. "Too bad he didn't have enough time to deliver presents to *our* house."

But when Jimmy went inside, he saw a big package under the tree . . . and it had his name on it!

Jimmy opened the package and found a small, glowing globe in a glass case.

“My dwarf star!” Jimmy exclaimed. Then he read the card. “‘To Jimmy: Sorry this is late. I had to let it cool for a couple of years. Your friend, Santa.’”

Carl and Sheen soon arrived to show Jimmy their presents.

"Look, Jimmy. Santa gave me peace on Earth," said Sheen, showing him the certificate.

"Look, Jimmy. Santa made me an honorary elf," said Carl.

"What did you get?" they wanted to know.

"Santa brought me the perfect decoration for the top of our tree," said Jimmy excitedly.

"We didn't think you believed in Santa, Jimmy," his parents said as Goddard placed the star on top of the Christmas tree.

"New data strongly suggests Santa definitely exists," Jimmy told them. "Merry Christmas, everyone!"